ROBBER ZOOM

Written by Hazel Townson
Illustrated by Philippe Dupasquier

GINN

Ziggy Zoom went back in time.

He saw a car.
The car had wheels.

He saw two men. They had no wheels.
The men went fast.

A police car went fast.

Ziggy went fast too.

They went fast round the corner.

They went fast round the market.

The police car went faster and faster and

the cars crashed!

The two men ran away.

Ziggy went after them.

He went past them.

He went zoom round the corner . . .

and stopped the men.

Everybody said, 'Well done, Ziggy Zoom!'